BRO/JF

First published 1983 by Julia MacRae Books
This edition published 1992 by Walker Books Ltd
87 Vauxhall Walk, London SE11 5HJ

12 14 16 18 20 19 17 15 13

© 1983 Anthony Browne

Printed in Hong Kong

British Library Cataloguing in Publication Data
A catalogue record for this title is
available from the British Library.
ISBN 0-86203-104-4

Gorilla